William C. Bennett

Baby May

and other poems on infants

William C. Bennett

Baby May
and other poems on infants

ISBN/EAN: 9783337397937

Printed in Europe, USA, Canada, Australia, Japan

Cover: Foto ©Andreas Hilbeck / pixelio.de

More available books at **www.hansebooks.com**

BABY MAY,

AND

OTHER POEMS ON INFANTS.

BY

W. C. BENNETT.

THIRD THOUSAND.

LONDON:

CHAPMAN AND HALL, 193, PICCADILLY.

1861.

TO

WILLIAM FREDERICK ROCK,

THIS LITTLE VOLUME

Is Inscribed,

WITH THE WARMEST ESTEEM AND REGARD,

BY HIS FRIEND,

W. C. BENNETT.

2, The Circus,
    Greenwich.

CONTENTS.

PREFACE.

TEN years since, "Baby May" was printed for private circulation; and I shortly after received a request from the late Mr. Douglas Jerrold that he might give it to the public in his "Shilling Magazine." It at once became a favourite. Since then it has been a pleasure to me to know that the little lady has made friends far and near, both in England and America; among whom she reckons with becoming pride, among the dead, Mary Russell Mitford, who re-introduced her to the public in her "Recollections of a Literary Life,"—among the living, Mr. John Ruskin, Mr. Nathaniel Hawthorne, Mr. and Mrs. Howitt, and many of the leading writers of England and America. The volume in which I published this best known of my poems is out of print, but I find that "Baby May" still holds her place in the recollections of her old acquaintances, and year by year gains new ones. It is recited in lectures, and included in American selections from the English poets ; and now I hear of constant requests that this and other poems of mine, on kindred subjects, may be reprinted at a price which will enable the many who wish for them to obtain them. So I again present her to the world, with a confident hope that her welcome may be as warm an one as that which so long since greeted her on her first appearance.

BABY MAY.

CHEEKS as soft as July peaches,
  Lips whose dewy scarlet teaches
Poppies paleness—round large eyes
Ever great with new surprise,
Minutes filled with shadeless gladness,
Minutes just as brimmed with sadness,
Happy smiles and wailing cries,
Crows and laughs and tearful eyes,
Lights and shadows swifter born
Than on wind-swept Autumn corn,
Ever some new tiny notion
Making every limb all motion—
Catchings up of legs and arms,
Throwings back and small alarms,
Clutching fingers—straightening jerks,
Twining feet whose each toe works,
Kickings up and straining risings,
Mother's ever new surprisings,
Hands all wants and looks all wonder
At all things the heavens under,
Tiny scorns of smiled reprovings
That have more of love than lovings,
Mischiefs done with such a winning
Archness, that we prize such sinning,

Breakings dire of plates and glasses,
Graspings small at all that passes,
Pullings off of all that's able
To be caught from tray or table;
Silences—small meditations,
Deep as thoughts of cares for nations,
Breaking into wisest speeches
In a tongue that nothing teaches,
All the thoughts of whose possessing
Must be wooed to light by guessing;
Slumbers—such sweet angel-seemings
That we'd ever have such dreamings,
Till from sleep we see thee breaking,
And we'd always have thee waking;
Wealth for which we know no measure,
Pleasure high above all pleasure,
Gladness brimming over gladness,
Joy in care—delight in sadness,
Loveliness beyond completeness,
Sweetness distancing all sweetness,
Beauty all that beauty may be,
That's May Bennett—that's my baby.

BABY'S SHOES.

O THOSE little, those little blue shoes!
   Those shoes that no little feet use!
      O the price were high,
      That those shoes would buy,
Those little blue unused shoes!

For they hold the small shape of feet
That no more their mother's eyes meet,
      That, by God's good will,
      Years since grew still,
And ceased from their totter so sweet!

And O, since that baby slept,
So hush'd! how the mother has kept,
      With a tearful pleasure,
      That little dear treasure,
And o'er them thought and wept!

For they mind her for evermore
Of a patter along the floor,
      And blue eyes she sees
      Look up from her knees,
With the look that in life they wore.

As they lie before her there,
There babbles from chair to chair
    A little sweet face,
    That's a gleam in the place,
With its little gold curls of hair.

Then O wonder not that her heart
From all else would rather part
    Than those tiny blue shoes
    That no little feet use,
And whose sight makes such fond tears start.

TODDLING MAY.

FIVE pearly teeth and two soft blue eyes,
 Two sinless eyes of blue,
That are dim or are bright they scarce know why,
 That, baby dear, is you.
And parted hair of a pale, pale gold,
 That is priceless, every curl,
And a boldness shy, and a fear half bold,
 Ay, that's my baby girl.

A small, small frock, as the snowdrop white,
 That is worn with a tiny pride,
With a sash of blue, by a little sight
 With a baby wonder eyed;
And a pattering pair of restless shoes,
 Whose feet have a tiny fall,
That not for the world's coined wealth we'd lose,
 That, Baby May, we call.

A rocker of dolls with staring eyes
 That a thought of sleep disdain,
That with shouts of tiny lullabies
 Are by'd and by'd in vain;
A drawer of carts with baby noise,
 With strainings and pursed-up brow,
Whose hopes are cakes and whose dreams are toys,
 Ay, that's my baby now.

A sinking of heart, a shuddering dread,
    Too deep for a word or tear,
Or a joy whose measure may not be said,
    As the future is hope or fear;
A sumless venture, whose voyage's fate
    We would and yet would not know,
Is she whom we dower with love as great
    As is perilled by hearts below.

Oh what as her tiny laugh is dear,
    Or our days with gladness girds!
Or what is the sound we love to hear
    Like the joy of her baby words!
Oh pleasure our pain, and joys our fears
    Should be, could the future say,
Away with sorrow—time has no tears
    For the eyes of Baby May.

CRADLE SONGS.

1.

LULLABY! O lullaby!
  Baby, hush that little cry!
    Light is dying,
    Bats are flying,
Bees to-day with work have done;
So, till comes the morrow's sun,
Let sleep kiss those bright eyes dry!
    Lullaby! O lullaby!

Lullaby! O lullaby!
Hushed are all things, far and nigh;
    Flowers are closing,
    Birds reposing,
All sweet things with life have done,
Sweet, till dawns the morning sun,
Sleep then kiss those blue eyes dry!
    Lullaby! O lullaby!

TO A LADY I KNOW, AGED ONE.

O SUNNY curls! O eyes of blue!
  The hardest natures known,
Baby, would softly speak to you,
  With strangely tender tone;
What marvel, Mary, if from such
  Your sweetness, love would call,
We love you, baby, O how much,
  Most dear of all things small!

Unborn, how, more than all on earth,
  Your mother yearn'd to meet
Your dream'd-of face; you, from your birth,
  Most sweet of all things sweet!
Even now for your small hands' first press
  Of her full happy breast,
How oft does she God's goodness bless,
  And feel her heart too blest!

You came, a wonder to her eyes,
  That doated on each grace,
Each charm that still with new surprise
  She show'd us in your face:

Small beauties? ah, to her not small,
  How plain to her blest mind!
Though, baby dear, I doubt if all,
  All that she found, could find.

A year has gone, and, mother, say,
  Through all that year's blest round,
In her, has one sweet week or day
  Not some new beauty found?
What moment has not fancied one,
  Since first your eyes she met?
And, wife, I know you have not done
  With finding fresh ones yet.

Nor I; for, baby, some new charm
  Each coming hour supplies,
So sweet, we think change can but harm
  Your sweetness in our eyes,
Till comes a newer, and we know
  As that fresh charm we see,
In you, sweet Nature wills to show
  How fair a babe can be.

Kind God, that gave this precious gift,
  More clung-to every day,
To Thee our eyes we trembling lift—
  Take not Thy gift away!
Looking on her, we start in dread,
  We stay our shuddering breath,
And shrink to feel the terror said
  In that one dark word—death.

O tender eyes! O beauty strange!
   When childhood shall depart,
O that thou, babe, through every change,
   May'st keep that infant heart!
O gracious God! O this make sure,
   That, of no grace beguiled,
The woman be in soul as pure
   As now she is, a child!

THE SEASONS.

A BLUE-EYED child that sits amid the noon,
   O'erhung with a laburnum's drooping sprays,
Singing her little songs, while, softly round,
   Along the grass the chequered sunshine plays.

All beauty that is throned in womanhood,
   Pacing a summer garden's fountained walks,
That stoops to smooth a glossy spaniel down,
   To hide her flushing cheek from one who talks.

A happy mother with her fair-faced girls,
   In whose sweet Spring again her youth she sees,
With shout and dance, and laugh, and bound, and song,
   Stripping an autumn orchard's laden trees.

An aged woman in a wintry room,
   Frost on the pane—without, the whirling snow;
Reading old letters of her far-off youth,
   Of pleasures past, and griefs of long ago.

TO A LOCKET.

O CASKET of dear fancies,
   O little case of gold,
What rarest wealth of memories
   Thy tiny round will hold!
With this first curl of baby's
   In thy small charge will live
All thoughts that all her little life
   To memory can give.

O prize its silken softness,
   Within its amber round
What worlds of sweet rememberings
   Will still by us be found;
The weak, shrill cry so blessing
   The curtained room of pain,
With every since-felt feeling
   To us 'twill bring again.

'Twill mind us of her lying
   In rest soft-pillowed deep,
While, hands the candle shading,
   We stole upon her sleep,

Of many a blessed moment
   Her little rest above
We hung in marvelling stillness,
   In ecstacy of love.

'Twill mind us, radiant sunshine
   For all our shadowed days,
Of all her baby wonderings,
   Of all her little ways.
Of all her tiny shoutings,
   Of all her starts and fears,
And sudden mirths out-gleaming
   Through eyes yet hung with tears.

There's not a care—a watching—
   A hope—a laugh—a fear,
Of all her little bringing,
   But we shall find it here;
Then, tiny golden warder,
   Oh safely ever hold
This glossy silken memory,
   This little curl of gold.

CRADLE SONGS.

2.

SLEEP! the bird is in its nest;
  Sleep! the bee is hushed in rest;
Sleep! rocked on thy mother's breast;
        Lullaby!
To thy mother's fond heart pressed,
        Lullaby!

Sleep! the waning daylight dies;
Sleep! the stars dream in the skies;
Daisies long have closed their eyes;
        Lullaby!
 Calm, how calm! on all things lies;
        Lullaby!

Sleep then, sleep! my heart's delight;
Sleep! and through the darksome night,
Round thy bed God's angels bright,
        Lullaby!
Guard thee till I come with light;
        Lullaby!

EPITAPHS FOR INFANTS.

1.

HERE Spring's tenderest nurslings set,
 Wind-flowers and the violet;
Here the white-drooped snowdrop frail,
And the lily of the vale;
All of sweetness passing soon,
Withering ere the year be noon;
For the little rester here,
Like these infants of the year,
Was, oh grief, as fair as they,
And as quickly fled away.

2.

Here the gusts of wild March blow
But in murmurs faint and low;
Ever here, when Spring is green,
Be the brightest verdure seen;
And when June's in field and glade,
Here be ever freshest shade.
Here hued Autumn latest stay,
Latest call the flowers away;
And when Winter's shrilling by,
Here its snows the warmest lie;
For a little life is here,
Hid in earth, for ever dear,
And this grassy heap above
Sorrow broods and weeping love.

3.

On this little grassy mound
Never be the darnel found:
Ne'er be venomed nettle seen
On this little heap of green;
For the little lost one here
Was too sweet for aught of fear,
Aught of harm to harbour nigh
This green spot where she must lie;
So be nought but sweetness found
On this little grassy mound.

4.

Here in gentle pity, Spring,
Let thy sweetest voices sing;
Nightingale, be here thy song
Charmed by grief to linger long;
Here the thrush with longest stay
Pipe its pleasant song to day,
And the blackbird warble shrill
All its passion latest still;
Still the old grey tower above
Her small rest, the swallow love,
And through all June's honied hours
Booming bees hum in its flowers,
And when comes the eve's cold gray
Murmuring gnats unresting play
Weave, while, round, the beetle's flight
Drones across the shadowing night;
For the sweetness dreaming here
Was a gladness to the year,
And the sad months all should bring
Dirges o'er her sleep to sing.

5.

Haunter of the opening year,
Ever be the primrose here;
Whitest daisies deck the spot,
Pansies and forget-me-not,
Fairest things that earliest fly,
Sweetness blooming but to die;
For this blossom, o'er whose fall
Sorrow sighs, was fair as all,
But, alas, as frail as they,
All as quickly fled away.

TO OUR BABY KATE.

A REVERIE.

MARVEL, baby, 'tis to me
   What thy little thoughts can be,
What the meanings small, that reach
Hearing in thy mites of speech,
Sayings that no language know
More than coo, and cry, and crow,
Would-be words, that hide away
All that they themselves would say,
Tiny fancies courting sight,
Maskéd from all in shrouding night;
Fain its secret I'd beguile
From the mystery of thy smile;
Fain would fathom all that lies
In thy pleasure and surprise,
In the fancies flitting through
Those two eyes of wondering blue,
In thy starts and tiny fears,
Gleams of joy and fleeting tears.
Ah, in vain I seek to win
Way to the small life within!
Curious thought no clue can find
To that wondrous world, thy mind,

That its little sights hath shown
Unto fancy's gaze alone ;
Therefore do I converse hold
Oft with fancy, to unfold
All the marvels of its seeing,
Wordless mysteries of thy being ;
Then of all seen things it tells
Unto thee, high miracles ;
How thy baby fancy lingers,
Wondering minutes o'er thy fingers,
Or, still marvelling more and more,
Eyes thy pinked feet o'er and o'er:
How the world and all things seem
Airy shadows of a dream,
Unsubstantial—forms unreal,
Out to which thy graspings feel
Wavering stretchings, marvelling much
At the mystery of a touch;
How with little shout thou'dst pass
To thy likeness in the glass,
Or thy little talks are told
Unto all thou dost behold,
Guessed-at griefs and baby joys
Crowed to busy sister's toys,
Or, in murmurings low, rehearsed
To the kitten for thee nursed.
So with fancy do I dream,
Baby mine, until I seem
All the little thoughts to know,
All thy little acts below,
Till thought comes and bids me own
That I dream and dream alone.

Yet one surety lies above
Reason's doubtings—thine is love,
Love abundant, leaping out
In thy lighted look and shout,
In thy joy that sorrow dumbs,
In thy bubbling laugh that comes
Ever still with glad surprise
When thy mother meets thine eyes.
Love is in thy eager watch
Ever strained her form to catch,
In thy glance that, place to place,
Tracks the gladness of her face,
In thy hush of joy that charms
Cries to stillness in her arms,
Calms of rapture, blessing, blest,
Rosy nestlings in her breast,
Dreaming eyes for ever raising
Raptured gazes to her gazing,
Gaze so blessed, sure we deem
Heaven is in thy happy dream.
So our love would have it be
Ever, little Kate, with thee;
Treasure, treasures all above,
Ever, baby, thine be love,
Love, that doubly-mirrored lives
In the smiles it wins and gives,
Love, that gives to life its worth,
Lending glory to the earth.

ON A DEAD INFANT.

DEAD! dead!—what peace abides within the word—
  For thee, O little one, what bliss of rest!
By her who bore thee, with what anguish heard,
    God knows!—God knoweth best;
God willeth best; yet while the words we say,
We know thy grief, wild mother, must have way.

Oh, never shall those tiny fingers press
Her cheek!—oh, never to the full breasts steal,
That yearn their tender touch, that so would bless,
    Their blessed touch to feel!
Oh, never shall those closed lids opening rise
To look delight into her hungering eyes!

Yearned for—how yearned for wast thou, little one!
Each month more dear that seemed to bring thee near,
Alas! that seemed, but seemed; God's will be done!
    We may not know thee here;
We may not know thee, but as, babe, thou art,
Cold even to thy mother's quivering heart.

Not know thee! Mother, with thy sorrow wild,
How is that still face stamped within thy heart!
That face so looked on, when, "Give me my child!"
    Thou criedst, nor dared we part
In that first moment from thy arms' embrace
The cold white stillness of that blind, fixed face.

God comfort her! all human words are vain
To bid her shun to die or care to live.
Who shall bid peace to be for her again?
      Who, save God, comfort give?
Who fill the empty heart that finds a void
In all it feared or hoped for or enjoyed?

God comfort her!—who else?—not even he
Who for thee, sweet one, bore a father's love,
Who, with what pride and joy! she looked to see
      Bend this new life above,
And show her in his eyes the unshadowed bliss
That looked from hers—alas! now changed to this!

Leave her to God and to the tender years
That soften misery into gentle grief,
Grief that may almost find at last from tears,
      Sad tears, may find relief,
Grief that from time may gather perfect trust
In all Heaven wills, and own even this is just.

For thee, dead snowdrop, all our tears are dried;
We know thee evermore as to us given
Within our hearts for ever to abide,
      Type of all meet for heaven;
Type of all purity of which we guess,
That heaven shall make more pure and earth not less.

Wake not! the cruel tender hand of death,
Death, with a tenderness for earth too deep,
Ere thou hadst drawn one mortal troubled breath,
      Hushed thee to quiet sleep,
Stilled, ere it woke, the anguish of thy cries,
Nor gave the tears of earth to dim thine eyes.

Why would we wake thee?—joy and grief, we know,
Walk hand in hand along earth's crowded ways;
Who 'scape the thorns that in our paths below
  For all life thickly lays?
Why should we wish thee on a weary way
Where thou might'st long for night while yet 'twas day?

For we, most blest, even when to heaven we turn
Eyes bright with thanks for all that makes life dear,
Even then our trembling hearts have not to learn
  Of sorrows that are here—
Of griefs that dimmed our dearest hours with tears—
Of bitter memories that seem shadowing fears.

Hope has no part in thee, in surety lost,
Sweet bud of being, but to bloom above;
Nor may our thoughts of thee with fear be crossed,
  Thou, homed in God's dear love,
Borne by thy heavenly Father's hand from all
That makes the purest stoop, the strongest fall.

Lily, thou shalt not know the soiling gust
Of earthly passion bow thee to its will;
Temptation and all ill are from thee thrust,
  Nor tears thine eyes shall fill;
Remorse and penitence thou shalt not need,
From sin's pollution and earth's errors freed.

Oh, blessed, to 'scape the mystery of life,
Its wavering walk 'twixt holiness and sin!
Allowed, without earth's struggles—our weak strife,
  Heaven's palms to win,
Through the bright portals thou at once hast pressed,
To endless blessedness and lasting rest.

CRADLE SONGS.

3.

LULLABY—lullaby, baby dear!
  Take thy rest without a fear;
Quiet sleep, for mother is here,
Ever wakeful, ever near,
        Lullaby!

Lullaby—lullaby! gone is the light,
Yet let not darkness my baby fright;
Mother is with her amid the night,
Then softly sleep, my heart's delight,
        Lullaby!

May thy small dreams no ill things see,
Kind Heaven keep watch, my baby, o'er thee,
Kind angels bright thy guardians be,
And give thee smiling to day and to me,
        Lullaby!

Sleep, sleep on! thy rest is deep;
But, ah! what wild thoughts on me creep,
As by thy side my watch I keep,
To think how like to death is sleep
        Lullaby!

But God our Father will hear my prayer,
And have thee, dear one, in His care;
Thee, little one, soft breathing there,
To me the Lord's dear love will spare,
        Lullaby!

Sleep on! sleep on! till glad day break,
And with the sunshine gladly wake,
Thy mother's day, how blest! to make,
Her life, what joy! through thy dear sake,
        Lullaby!

THE WISH.

MY boy, my boy, what would I have
　　Thy future lot should be,
Were that sweet fay, so kind of old,
　　To leave the choice with me?
Were she to say, " My fairy power,
　　To grant all blessings, use;
Give what thou wilt to this young life,
　　And what thou wilt, refuse."

Her diamond wand, my little one,
　　Above thee would I raise,
" Be health," I'd say, "be beauty thine,
　　My boy, through all thy days.
The perfect powers that give thee strength
　　Thy work on earth to do;
The perfect form, that shows the soul's
　　Own beauty shining through.

" Be plenty thine; that, wealthy, thou
　　Mayst independent live;
That, rich, to thee it may be given
　　Abundantly to give:
That heaven, through means of that thou hast,
　　To thee may be made sure;
In life—in death—that thou mayst have
　　The blessings of the poor.

" Be thine a warm and open heart,
　　Be thine unnumbered friends;
A life, held precious while it lasts,
　　And wept for when it ends.

And, heaven on earth, be thine a home
　　Where children round thee grow,
Where one, with all thy mother's love,
　　Makes blest thy days below.

" Harold, be thine that better life
　　That higher still aspires,
Supreme in sovereign sway above
　　The senses' low desires ;
And thine the fame that, told of, men
　　Of holy deeds shall hear,
A glory, unto good men's thoughts
　　And lowly memories dear.

" Walk thou a poet among men,
　　A prophet sent of God,
That hallowed grow the common ways
　　Of earth, which thou hast trod ;
That truth in thy eternal words
　　Sit throned in might sublime,
And love and mercy, from thy tongue,
　　For ever preach to Time.

" All human wishes most desire,
　　All last they would resign,
All fondest love can long to give,
　　My little one, be thine.
The purest good that man can know,
　　To thee, my boy, be given ;
And be thy every act on earth
　　A deed, to win thee heaven ! "

TO W. G. B.

SOUL, not yet from heaven beguiled,
  Soul, not yet by earth defiled,
Dwelling in this little child,
    Be, O to him be
    All we would have thee!

Through this life of joy and care,
If that grief must be his share,
Make, O make him strong to bear
    All God willeth, all
    That to him must fall.

O when passions stir his heart,
Tempting him from good to part,
Make him from the evil start,
    That he walk aright,
    Soil-less in God's sight!

Taint him not with mortal sin,
That heaven's palms his hands may win,
That heaven's gates he enter in,
    Of God's favour sure,
    Pure as he is pure!

If he wander from the right,
O through error's darksome night,
On to heaven's eternal light,
    Guide, O guide his way
    To heaven's perfect day!

CRADLE SONGS.

4.

SLEEP, boy, sleep—sleep!
  For the day is for waking—for rest the night,
And my boy must learn to use each aright;
    Let him toil in the day, and steep
Through the night his senses in slumber sound,
To fit him to work when day comes round!
    Sleep, boy, sleep—sleep!

    Sleep, boy, sleep—sleep!
For my boy must be strong of body and limb,
To do all I'd have to be done by him;
    Let his slumbers be sound and deep,
That stout of arm and of heart he may grow,
Both hot to do and keen to know;
    Sleep, boy, sleep—sleep!

    Sleep, boy, sleep—sleep!
For no puny son must I have—not I,
Made through his days but to crouch and sigh,
    To bend and to weakly weep;
No—my man must be strong to battle with care,
The bravest to do, and the boldest to dare;
    Sleep, boy, sleep—sleep!

    Sleep, boy, sleep—sleep!
Yes, thy mother, my boy, would have thee one
By whom this old world's best work is done;
    One who on its dullards shall sweep,   [strife,
If it must be, through storm—if it must be, through
To still freer thoughts, and to still purer life;
    Sleep, boy, sleep—sleep!

THE STORY OF A MOTHER.

FROM HANS CHRISTIAN ANDERSEN.

THERE the little one lay, white and dying,
  And beside its bed, with sorrow wild,
Wailed the mother, unto Heaven crying,
  " Spare my baby ! spare, O God, my child ! "

Then the darkness, death, arose before her,
  Laid its hand upon her baby's heart ;
And, a nameless anguish creeping o'er her,
  From her infant saw she life depart.

It was dead, and fixed before her eye was
  That dear face that on her should have smiled ;
But a moment dumb with grief, her cry was
  Straight, " O God ! O give me back my child ! "

Then it was as if God willed to send her
  Answer to the wail that from her rose ;
And it seemed as if, with accents tender,   [close ! "
  Death breathed, " Fate, what might have been, dis-

And with anguish that she might not smother,
  Looked she through the distant years with awe,
All the child had lived to, saw the mother ;
  All its grown-up life the mother saw.

And she saw her babe, her heart's dear treasure,
    Fated, not to peace and joy, alas!
Fated, not to know a pure life's pleasure,
    But through want, and woe, and guilt to pass.

Then the mother knew her human blindness,
    And, even through her tears, she brightly smiled,
" Blessed be God! " she cried. " that in His kindness,
    Bore from earth, and sin, and shame, my child ! "

CRADLE SONGS.

5.

SLEEP, baby, sleep!
  Cease thy bitter crying!
In the cold earth deep,
Deep in death's long sleep,
O that we were lying!
  Sleep, baby, sleep!

Sleep, baby, sleep!
Let's forget to-morrow
  Comes, when we must bear
  Scorn, and want, and care,
Waking but for sorrow!
  Sleep, baby, sleep!

Sleep, baby, sleep!
Thy poor mother pity!
  Worn and faint, she hears
  No voice her life that cheers
In all this great, hard city;
  Sleep, baby, sleep!

Sleep, baby, sleep!
Thou hast thy mother only;
  Cold and still lies he
  Who worked for thee and me,
And left us, boy, how lonely!
  Sleep, baby, sleep!

Sleep, baby, sleep!
Faint and, God! how weary!
Let these eyes, how blest!
Baby mine, in rest,
Forget this world so dreary!
Sleep, baby, sleep!

Sleep, baby, sleep!
Heed not mother's crying!
O boy, by God's will,
We were cold and still,
With thy father lying!
Sleep, baby, sleep!

Fcap. 8vo., cloth, 3s. 6d.,

QUEEN ELEANOR'S VENGEANCE,

And other Poems.

London : CHAPMAN & HALL, 193, Piccadilly.

From the Critic.

" We look upon Mr. Bennett as a landmark to indicate the way where lie the strength of nature and the power of simplicity. He is one of those old-fashioned poets—rare now, and valuable from their rarity—who were not ashamed to speak naturally like men, and who evinced power without the exhibition of muscular throes. As a poem, 'Queen Eleanor's Vengeance' is admirable; it has the intensity of tragic fire It is brief, but pointed and defined as a poniard.   In conspicuous contrast to this poem we would place another, entitled ' A New Griselda.' Here there is simplicity of style, but neither bareness nor barrenness. The tender emotions, which are best known to those who dive deepest below the surface of domestic life, are employed in this poem as only a true poet can employ them. Mr. Bennett's great triumphs, in our opinion, consist not in the kingly manner in which he walks the classic regions of the 'Gods,' but in the homely step which carries him through the dwellings of men.   He is known—and it is a pleasing acknowledgment of his fame to say so—by thousands of little happy folk, wingless, but no less on that account our nursery angels, and by thousands of full-grown men and women. No wonder he is so well known, since he has conversed with them in a language they can understand—since he has expressed to them home delights and home sorrows with the purest Saxon feeling. The volume before us will serve still more, to rivet the fellowship of the poet and his readers."

From Fraser's Magazine.

" It is impossible to deny the genuine pictorial power of the mind from which this description, that might stand for a translation into words of Titian's ' Bacchus and Ariadne,' in our National Gallery, proceeds......Perhaps a famous song of Shelley's may have been echoing in Mr. Bennett's brain when he wrote this ' Summer Invocation;' but no one that was not a true poet could have reproduced the echo with such a sweet melody, and such delicate touches of his own.   Altogether, Mr. Bennett's volume appears to us full of promise."

From the Athenæum.

"Many a tender thought and charming fancy find graceful utterance in his pages."

From the Examiner.

"Mr. W. C. Bennett shares with Dr. Mackay the right to be popular on the score of simple, unaffected utterance. In his new volume we like the natural tone of the 'New Griselda,' better than the ballad style—less suited to the writer's genius—of the 'Queen Eleanor's Vengeance,' after which the book is named. But there is everywhere unexaggerated expression, a pleasant sense of the joy of the primrose bank, of blooming thorn-trees, and of summer rain; and there is occasional expression of that love of children, which few writers of our day have expressed with so much naïve fidelity as Mr. Bennett."

From the Weekly Dispatch.

"Mr. W. C. Bennett is a poet of great power, and possessing a fine descriptive faculty, especially when employed on subjects of a picturesque, rural character. Some of his poems on children, too, are among the most charming in the language, and are familiar in a thousand homes. The longest poem in the book is 'Queen Eleanor's Vengeance,' a terrible tale, related with commensurate force. 'Pygmalion' is an ambitions strain, finely conceived and executed. Mr. Bennett has produced a charming and graceful book."

From the Guardian.

"Mr. Bennett writes with practised skill, and what is more remarkable in these days, with unimpeachable taste. He is a man of taste and ability, who will yield pleasure and interest to every one who reads him."

From the National Magazine.

"Another volume has proceeded from the pen of Mr. W. C. Bennett. It is entitled 'Queen Eleanor's Vengeance, and other Poems.' Among these there are strains that bring Tennyson and Browning to mind, without abating our respect for the immediate author. The ballad which initiates the collection is written in stanza-couplets, and shows a power in dealing with the elements of the terrible perhaps not suspected by the author's admirers. On the Fair Rosamond he dwells but little; the vindictive feelings of the jealous Eleanor are those that have plainly fascinated the poet's genius. A dramatic poem, entitled 'A Character,' manifests the same tendency. The Creole, Lina Merton, is a Queen Eleanor on a small scale, and of a more metaphysical turn of mind; but her vengeance is equally cruel, or rather more so. The Queen only murders, but the Creole annihilates. The piece, however, most to our mind, is 'The Boat Race.' The 'New Griselda,' which is evidently the writer's favourite, has less of pure beauty, and the conventions introduced disturb the ideal impressions. Mr. Bennett's classic imitations are, as usual, excellent. Theocritus writes again in such pieces as 'Pygmalion,' 'Ariadne,' and 'The Judgment of Midas.' The political pieces are vigorous, satirical, and fully justify the reputation already acquired by the author for compositions of the kind. But it is in his domestic moods that we best love to encounter Mr. Bennett. Is not the following ('Baby's Shoes') exquisite? Among the more ambitious efforts, we may note with especial commendation the poems entitled 'Columbus,' and the 'Star of the Ballet.' The last is a ballad, in which simplicity, thought. and sentiment wrestle for the victory, and lovingly unite, as it were, in a war embrace."

Fcap. 8vo., cloth, 3s. 6d.,

SONGS BY A SONG-WRITER.

First Hundred.

London : CHAPMAN & HALL, 193, Piccadilly.

From the Leader.

"Mr. W. C. Bennett has been well-advised to collect his various songs. The only difficulty that could be in his way was their number. He has endeavoured to solve this by experimenting, first of all, with a specimen of his quality. He has selected from his large store a hundred; and here they are, in a handsome volume, which ought immediately to become popular. We find here many old acquaintances, and some new faces; but everywhere the same grace, melody, and Saxon purity of language. A little more accuracy and finish, and Mr. Bennett might rank as the Béranger of England. Here we find the sweet song of 'Baby's Shoes,' on which Miss Mitford bestows such high commendation, and which has been so frequently quoted with enthusiastic recognition; and that Béranger-like 'London Lyric, from a Garret,' which so rationally and heroically moralises on the distinction between true and false riches, and defies poverty altogether. To this we would add 'The Dressmaker's Thrush.' Fine, too, is the song inscribed 'To the Memory of Robert Burns,' a just tribute from one whose own writings reflect so much of the influences derived from those of the Scottish bard. It is one of the most ambitious poems in the collection. Other poems of Mr. Bennett show, in lyrical form, a fine degree of political shrewdness, and a scorn of mere partial prejudices, whether national or social. Witness those capital 'Friendly Hints to Transatlantic Friends,' which he has headed with 'God save the Queen.' For the most part, Mr. Bennett's songs deal with facts, the stern, hard facts of the Mammon-ridden world; but there are, nevertheless, some most delicious fancies scattered between. Mr. Bennett has borrowed largely from our old poets, and sometimes indulges freely in their wildest conceits. His mind is not simply a mirror, purely reflecting nature and society, but he has coloured it with innumerable associations, both ancient and modern; so that his subjects always derive some attributes from the media through which he perceives them. Though a self-taught, he is a highly-educated writer, and to some extent, therefore, his treatment of his themes is artificial; there is, however, always a basis of originality in all he writes, for he is not a mere mocking-bird, but a genuine poet."

From the Literary Gazette.

" He bids fair to become one of our best English song-writers."

From the Athenæum.

"On reading this book we are glad to find that Mr. Bennett is himself again. We always like his writing when he dares to be true to his own genius. The stream of his verse is not a deep-flowing one, but it is clear and healthy; it runs with a sprightly music, and there often flutters such a dance of sunbeams on the surface, that we do not think of gauging the depth. Here is a song with a minuet movement, and a conscious seventeenth-century kind of grace. This soft, sweet murmuring invocation to the summer rain is one we like."

From the Critic.

" Mr. Bennett comes before us in his hundred songs—only an instalment, these—with qualifications which admirably adapt him to his work. In his poems, which have demanded constructive power, which a song, strictly speaking, does not, he has shown two of the conditions without which song cannot exist. These are melody and naturalness. We hold Mr. Bennett to be among the best of our song-writers. There is fire in his patriotic, and tenderness in his domestic themes. What a sweet picture, and what homely pathos there is in ' The Daisy.' And what more joyous than this 'Spring Song?' For a truthful, heart-gushing strain, we should quote 'The Dressmaker's Thrush.' What a world-wide sermon lives in that regretful refrain! We hope Mr. Bennett will give the world the remainder of his songs. He is so genial, so healthy, so purely Saxon, that silence on his part would go far to favour the growth of literary spasm and contortion."

From the Illustrated Times.

"Mr. Bennett is quite right in calling himself a writer of songs. Nearly all the lyric poetry contained in this volume is admirable, but the songs are particularly beautiful. Some of the poems about children (especially the charming one entitled 'Baby's Shoes,') are as good as anything of the kind that has ever been written; and Mr. Bennett's verse is always flowing and melodious, but, on the whole, he is more a song-writer than anything else. When he writes in his own simple, natural way, we have no song-writer who can be compared to him."

From the Atlas.

"We opened this volume with serious misgivings, which passed away before we had read three pages. Mr. Bennett has achieved a most decided success; his songs as poems will cling fast to the reader's mind, and if only they be joined to fitting music, the author may look forward to a popularity almost as great as Dibdin ever enjoyed. We could only wish that he had himself written his lyrics to some of the old favourite tunes, which are at present in the company of very bad words. Mr. Bennett is a man of all moods. Here is a pretty love-song, ('A Sailor's Song.') which none can read and not admire. In the piece entitled 'The Tricolor,' we have an appeal to our patriotism. Its vigour and melody of rhythm carry the reader along as if to the sound of martial music. Beautifully contrasted, and thoughtfully worked-out are the ideas in the only two songs which we have space to quote, 'The Homeward Watch,' and 'The Wrecked Hope.'"

From the John Bull.

"This author has established such general fame as a song-writer, that few writers have achieved similar popularity. The present 'first hundred' compositions are conceived in the purest and most versatile vein of poetry, and if their reception does not encourage successive centuries of verse, we shall be much mistaken."

From the Statesman.

"Mr. Bennett's volume contains a hundred songs, many of them of great merit. 'Song-writer' is an ambitious title, but Mr. Bennett has vindicated his right to a place of some note among those to whom it may be applied."

From the Morning Herald.

"Mr. Bennett is already known to the English reading public as a poet of much ability. He is extremely happy in his descriptions of pastoral and domestic life. He possesses real poetic feeling, and we are glad to add, his sentiments are always English, and they are sure to find a response in the hearts of his countrymen and countrywomen. He has written nearly 400 songs. Most of those in the volume now published are very good indeed. Many are really beautiful."

From the Inquirer.

"Mr. Bennett's stirring war-songs and occasional contributions to newspapers and magazines have made their writer widely known as a popular poet. Like most good songs, some of the lighter strains in the volume before us need to be wedded to suitable music in order to be fully appreciated; but in the graver pieces we discern a deep sympathy with humanity and a fervid sentiment of patriotism which entitle their author to a high place among our popular song-writers. Mr. Bennett does not belong to the servile horde of imitators, but writes with a vigour of thought and a graceful clearness of style which are peculiarly his own. The following pathetic lines ('The Wife's Appeal,') for the sake of the powerful influence they are calculated to exercise in a good cause, if for no other reason, deserve as wide a circulation as can possibly be given to them."

From the News of the World.

"'Ever since I could read songs,' says Mr. Bennett, 'I have loved them,' and we may add, that ever since he began to write them the public have been pleased with what he has written. In this volume we have a hundred charming things, which will delight all readers, because of their true feeling and unaffected grace."

From the Weekly Dispatch.

"Mr. Bennett has collected into a neat volume a century of songs, and promises more. This fertility would be alarming in a writer of feeble powers, but Mr. Bennett writes so freshly and charmingly that we always read his poems with pleasure. He writes like a true poet, especially on domestic subjects, or when sketching landscapes, with a feeling akin to that of Creswick or Lee. We are bound to say that his political songs have a vigour such as few poets can infuse One, indeed, 'The Tricolor,' might, if wedded to kindred music, become another 'Marseillaise.'"

From the Observer.

"The author of these songs has a considerable fund of poetry in his nature, and has written several songs which deserve to be popular. One of them, 'The Dressmaker's Thrush,' is of the right stuff, and will doubtless obtain admiration. This volume ought to meet with public favour, more particularly as the feeling which animates its contents is true."

From the Morning Star.

"Many of these songs would inspire us to wish that Mr. Bennett may be induced to appear soon again in print. One of the best songs in the book is to the memory of Béranger; another, to the memory of Robert Burns, is of nearly equal merit. There are several of the songs we should like to quote, but must refer our readers to the volume itself, and we feel sure that those who have a taste for this particular kind of poetry will find much that is pleasing and original."

From the Daily Telegraph.

"From the poems published in the present volume, we should select ' The Tricolor,' as pre-eminently dist.nguished for vigour and that melodious ring of rhyme which thrills the heart through the ear, making the pulses beat to the march of verse as to warlike music. There is pith and irresistible humour in his ' Hints to Transatlantic Friends.' But Mr. Bennett speaks to the heart not only through the heroic chanson or sparkling satire; not less effective are those fragments appealing to the social and domestic feelings. In these we perceive a tender grace, a pathos and a charm, which offer a refreshing contrast to the prosaic monotony usually characterizing effusions of this class. This truthfulness to nature, hearty simplicity of utterance, and sportive play of fancy, it is which enables Mr. Bennett so well to adapt the poetic art to the events and emotions of ordinary life. To beautify and elevate these through the transfiguration of poetry, is, we think, essentially Mr. Bennett's vocation, though he has proved himself to possess unmistakeable capacity for minstrelsy of another order."

From the Sunday Times.

"He possesses, in no small degree, the qualities which this species of composition requires—feeling, fancy, condensation, and a varied power of expression."

From the Weekly Times.

"He is terse, epigrammatic, and can be, when he pleases, eloquent and pathetic."

From the Morning Advertiser.

"Varied in sentiment and style, some of the compositions display much force, feeling, and taste. The volume will be acceptable to a vast number of readers—those to whom the song sings to the heart. We can heartily commend Mr. Bennett's songs to our readers."

From the Morning Chronicle.

"This volume of a hundred songs by Mr. Bennett will be a welcome addition to the poetic literature of the day."

NEW VOLUME,

Just Published, foolscap 8vo., 3s. 6d.

THE WORN WEDDING-RING,

And other Poems.

From the *Morning Chronicle.*

"Mr. Bennett has unquestionably won the right of being reckoned with the poets of his country. At present he is the poet of the home and its affections. His 'Baby May and other Poems on Infants' broke entirely new ground; it was found that we had a singer amongst us able to touch our hearts on the tenderest side. His 'Baby's Shoes' was hailed as a poem perfect of its kind, and sure of admiration as long as fathers and mothers shall continue to love their children, or children remain the lovely things that God has made them. In the round of English poetry there are no lyrics that are so thoroughly imbued with the spirit of childhood as those of Mr. Bennett. But it is not only as the poet of childhood that Mr. Bennett has won his well-deserved popularity. It has been said of him, that with a very little more of accuracy and finish he might fairly be called the Béranger of England. There is, undoubtedly, a remarkable similarity of power evinced by Mr. Bennett in his songs; they come nearer to the heart-stirring strains of the great French lyrist than any songs of the day.

"In the volume before us the excellence of Mr. Bennett's songs is very conspicuous. They have all the qualities requisite to make them popular, and, like those which he has before published, they will doubtless be heartily received by the public. Full of vigour, freshness, music, and feeling, they are worthy to be on every lip. 'The Worn Wedding-ring,' which gives its title to the present volume, is a little poem, full of grace, tenderness, and piety, in which the sight of his wife's worn wedding-ring calls up in the poet's mind the history of all the joys, sorrows, and cares that have passed over them both, since the time 'when this old ring was new.' Some of the sonnets are decidedly fine, reminding us of Wordsworth, and even of Milton."

From the *Literary Gazette.*

"Many of the Sonnets are equal, after their kind, to his best songs. Many are as fresh, thoughtful, and musical as any that have appeared since Wordsworth thought and wrote. Of the earlier part of Mr. Bennett's volume we can only remark, to those who know that he is great in songs, that he here well sustains his reputation. We would, in conclusion, say of Mr. Bennett, that we hope he will always give us such a Christmas-box. 'Baby May' was, perhaps, more charming in its simplicity than anything in the present volume, but the old graceful homeliness and pathos are fully evidenced here."

From the Spectator.

"'The Worn Wedding-ring' is one of the prettiest poems by the author of 'Baby May.' It expresses, in simple and enthusiastic verses, the genuine feeling of a man who has been married many years to a wife he has always loved. This is a good subject for a poem, because it is common human ground for feeling. Mr. W. C. Bennett is a sweet singer of the people; to our thinking, one of the very best among those who use 'the Doric strain.' His domestic poems and songs of every-day life would have found favour with Wordsworth, for the sake of their love of nature and power of appreciating all the small goods of life."

From the Critic.

"There is an earnest simplicity about Mr. Bennett which gives him a high place among our modern poets."

From the Globe.

"The poem which gives a title to this volume is in the happiest style of the writer, who is established as the poet of heart and home. 'The Worn Wedding-ring' is a fitting address to the mother of 'Baby May.' Similarly illustrative of the hold which home association has over Mr. Bennett, is his address to his 'Native Town.' 'Leafy Greenwich, green pleasant Greenwich' is sung in the most taking homely ballad style, such as Isaac Walton would have loved to hear 'maidens singing over their milking-pails.'"

From the Illustrated Times.

"Mr. Bennett is now well known, and cordially accepted as a writer of songs and of child-poetry; and the songs in this new volume are most of them very welcome and pleasant reading. The refrains are capitally managed."

From the London American.

"Mr. Bennett's happiest efforts are those in which he deals with the social affections. He certainly has the power to enwrap the feelings while he charms the imagination. A sort of pastoral simplicity breathes through his odes, bringing the freshness of the country into town, as witness the following on Greenwich. But with all the gentleness breathing in this and kindred compositions, Mr. Bennett has a reserved power which reminds us, in its occasional manifestations, of some of the grandest strains of Schiller and Goethe."

From the Morning Advertiser.

"Mr. Bennett is equally happy in his descriptions of rural beauty, the pleasures of the country, and the sublimity of the ocean. The book altogether will be decidedly popular with the lovers of poetry."

From the Weekly Dispatch.

" A new volume of poems by Mr. Bennett is sure of a welcome. Few of our writers are so happy in the exhibition of the domestic feelings, the pure and intense love of a good man for the wife and children whose presence at the domestic fire-side imparts its dearest charm. Without obtruding personal relationships, Mr. Bennett sounds a note of natural emotion, to which all must respond; and this is the reason of the great popularity of his child-poems. Natural and unaffected, playful and tender, they are almost unequalled for their understanding of child nature,—a most delightful thing, though a great mystery to some. But Mr. Bennett is not alone a poet of the domestic affections. He can raise a louder and loftier strain, on the side of freedom and progress, and sketch, with rare felicity, the aspects of nature, especially in rural scenes. The volume before us contains specimens of all the aspects of his muse; and we recognize one or two sonnets, especial favourites of ours, which well deserved the reprint."

From the English Churchman.

" We have before had occasion to praise Mr. Bennett as worthy to rank amongst the best of our modern song-writers. The volume which he now puts forward forms another instalment of miscellaneous pieces and sonnets, all of them embodying graceful thoughts in pleasant verse, and each in its turn exhibiting the versatility of the writer,—the pathetic, the stirring, the earnest and the quaint following each other in quick succession throughout the volume. We cordially recommend it to notice."

From the Atlas.

"These poems have refreshed and delighted us."

From the John Bull.

" Mr. Bennett has before this established his fame as a popular poet. 'The Worn Wedding-ring' and the 'Green Hills of Surrey' are specimens of Mr. Bennett's very best style in the way of songs, both happily rendering true human emotion in musical and vigorous lines. We like his sonnets better than his songs; there is something in the mood of his poetry which suits the form of the sonnet, and he has especial strength in illustrating by this medium the higher aspect of art. We may cite particularly, in evidence of this, his sonnet on 'Holman Hunt's Picture,' and that on the 'Tomb of Benozzo Gozzoli.' His beautiful sonnet on the 'Venus de Medici' is conceived in a far higher vein of poetry than the sensuous stanza of Childe Harold on the same subject; and among many that will make the name of their author live, we may point especially to those on 'The Turners,' 'The Photograph of Dante,' and 'To Keats.'"

From the National Magazine.

"Mr. Bennett has again come before the world with a volume of poems. To the readers of the 'National' it is superfluous to expatiate on his merits. We all love him as the poet of home and its treasures. No one has sung so well of the joy, and beauty, and blessedness of childhood—of the sacred tie which binds together man and wife—of the tenderness which grows and ripens, and bears fruit by the fireside. His verse is always harmonious, healthy, and cheering; and we feel all the better after reading his songs. Some of his very sweetest are in the volume whose title we have just given, and, besides, we have many noble sonnets, in simplicity and dignity almost rivalling those of Wordsworth. Let us trust he may go on singing, and the world listening, for many coming years. When such poems as these are in demand it is a good sign of the times."

From the Eclectic Review.

"Mr. Bennett's volume is born of a reverent and loving spirit, enjoying the world, and especially the social affections of the English fireside. Mr. Bennett's poems are well-known by us, and we have before now said our hearty commendatory word upon them; they are the productions of a happy, cheerful nature, to whom life has brought all its best things, and taken few away. His verses, so flowing along like a merry brook, occasionally detained, it may be, for a few moments, and compelled to wear upon its wavelets a deeper shadow from some overhanging tree, or brooding village, or darker bay, but hastening on again, as fast as possible, into the open space, the sunshine, and the buoyant air and light; a hearty appreciation of all graceful and beautiful things—not merely the cold critical eye to perceive, but the heart to feel beauty as well, for whom travel has done a little, and books more. Happy husband, happy father, lively and free, in his, no doubt, happy home, and with no disposition to see the dark things of life. We do not think that this volume will add to Mr. Bennett's reputation: certainly it will not diminish it. We have no baby poetry here; and Mr. Bennett is the acknowledged and crowned laureate of babies. He has a fine eye for nature—lines of very graphic description—description which shows heart-work and artist-work are here. He has also a fine eye for art; he has also, which in these days is a more rare faculty, reverence before noble men and teachers."